20 Paces: The Four Revenants

By Marcus E.T.

Table of Contents

The Old West, Circa 1877

It was still early morning in Wisdom Peak.

Wesley Winchester polished off the last section of his bar counter. Fortunately, it was an easy morning and he only had to clean up around a few idlers who were passed out from the previous night. His teenaged daughter, Whitney, was helping him by replacing the chairs in their proper positions and resetting the tables.

He expected the first wave of the regular drunks to enter at any moment, but he didn't expect to see a new face, and an intimidating one at that. A middle-aged man dressed in black, with intense eyes, long dark hair, and a grisly, scarred visage indicating long days under the desert sun and a life driven by violence. The stranger adjusted his coat and belt at the door, giving Wesley a glimpse of the bandoleer across his chest and the two revolvers that hung from either hip. A long knife was also tucked into his belt.

Whitney froze at the sight of the man as he entered and approached the bar. She was not directly in his line of sight, but he seemed to smirk at her reaction, amused by frightening the young woman.

Wesley noted the way the man walked. His steps were measured. His palms remained open and close to his holstered weapons. His shoulders were straight, like he'd never relaxed a day in his life. This man was always ready for a fight. Wesley could feel some sense of wickedness emanating from this stranger as they locked eyes and the newcomer took a seat at the bar, folding his grimy hands on the counter.

"Hey there," Wesley said. "What can I get for you?"

 "Just information," the stranger said with a hard drawl. "I hear the sheriff of this town has established order 'round here for close to a decade... And I also hear he cleaned up the whole town without even using a gun. Izzat true?"

"That's right. He only uses his mind. Guns in Wisdom Peak are banned since he became the protector and law here. You would do best to stow yours away if you intend to leave here with them.”

“I intend to leave this town with much more than what I came here with” the stranger said, giving a grim grin as he turned his head slightly to glance over his shoulder toward Whitney. “And you say *protector*?” He spat out the last word.

“That’s right,” Wesley said moving a few feet down the bar, busying himself with inspecting glasses to create some distance between himself and the man. “He enforces the law and order here and fights on behalf of all of us.”

“I heard he’s some kind of legend who took out a band of looters who came through here some years back?”

“You heard that right, too. The townspeople here had weapons then and a different sheriff. Lots of people, including the old sheriff, were killed, but the young man who would become our current sheriff repelled them all. None of the invaders survived...”

"So, what is his weapon of choice then? No gun, so he likes knives? Cannons? Poison?"

"No. He only uses his mind. He's... *gifted.*"

The stranger's jaw tensed. He grinded his teeth, sighed and slowly stood. His hands suddenly moved with such speed, even Wesley's eyes could not follow. In an instant, both hands came back up onto the counter, both holding the revolvers Wesley noticed before. The man settled back onto the barstool he was on, keeping one revolver trained on Wesley and the other lying flat on the counter.

"You're really not giving me much to go on here," the stranger said. "Now, *I asked for information.* You've only told me what I already know. So, let me tell you who I am. The name is Mickey McGraw. You heard of me?"

Wesley nodded. "The undefeated gunslinger, known as the "Grim Gun" because you slay every man with a single shot, as easily as the Grim Reaper wielding his scythe."

"That's right," Mickey said, grinning and doing his best impression of Wesley's voice. "And by your own words, you said you don't have a single weapon in this town to defend yourself with? That the only person who could protect you in this whole place is your sheriff? So, by your own word, unless the sheriff were here right now, between you, those three drunks behind me and that pretty young thang back there, there would be no one who could stop me from shooting any one of you in the face and walking out of here?"

Wesley licked his lips. He knew a day like this would come. He'd prepared for it since the new sheriff had come to town. He just needed time to get to...

"Excuse me," a voice said from the entrance doorway.

Mickey spun on his barstool to find a young man, probably in his mid-twenties, smartly dressed, lean but firmly built, and clean-shaven. What stood out most of all was the dark complexion of this man and the shiny badge on his chest. The young man had no coat to conceal anything. Mickey could plainly see he was unarmed.

Mickey nodded casually, but squinted and twisted his mouth in disdain. "Sheriff?"

"Sir," the sheriff said sauntering over toward Mickey, who still had one gun trained on Wesley's chest. "I was told there was a newcomer to my town, and I'm guessing that would be you. I don't know if anyone has told you yet, but guns are not permitted in—"

"Yeah," Mickey said flatly. "I was told. I just don't care."

Mickey holstered his weapons and stood up from the stool.

"If you can't abide by the laws here, like anywhere else, you can leave or spend some time in a jail," the sheriff said, shrugging nonchalantly.

Mickey snickered as he strolled over to the young sheriff. "Ain't you a polite one? Don't see too many who look like you wearing clothes like that or a badge. You *must be* some kind of magic negro or conman to have authority over a whole town. Huh, little nig—?"

"*That word* is banned here, too," the young man said with only a hint of agitation in his voice as he met Mickey's eyes defiantly. "Now, are you going to hand over your weapons?"

"No," Mickey said, now standing directly in front of the sheriff, only a foot from his face. He stood a head taller than the dark-skinned boy and looked down not only to make eye contact, but so that his dank breath assailed the sheriff's nostrils and his spittle flew into the shorter man's face. "But you can give me something. That is if you want me to leave here peacefully..."

"What's that?" the boy said, unflinching. "Hygiene tips?"

Mickey chuckled before hocking some phlegm and attempting to spit on the sheriff's badge pinned to Black man's chest. To his surprise, just as the loogie was ejected from his lips, it suddenly leapt back into his mouth, splattering against his own rotted teeth and gums.

The sheriff didn't even flinch. The barmaid who watched quietly from the corner suddenly erupted into laughter.

"I want two hundred and twelve pounds in gold and food loaded into the cart hooked up to the horses out front," Mickey snarled as he wiped the spit from his mouth. "Get that and I will be on my way."

The sheriff never broke eye contact. The boy had nerve.

"No, you would just keep coming back," the sheriff said firmly. "Guys like you never stay away if people just give you what you think you're entitled to."

"Yeah, I hoped you would say that," Mickey said, his rotten grin growing wider now. "I like to give people the choice between giving me my weight in valuables or a duel... I think killing you would be much more valuable than whatever trash these people could offer me to leave."

"And how's that?"

"Well, like me, you're kind of a legend. I don't much like legends. I also don't like mouthy spooks who don't know their place. What's your name, boy?"

"Wisdom."

Mickey laughed. "Dumber than I thought. I asked for your name, not the town's."

The young man shrugged. "I take no offense to having my intelligence insulted by someone with the mental acuity of a horseshoe. My name is *Wisdom Armstrong*. People call me Wiz for simplicity. You could too if it's too hard for you to say. Simple seems to be your nature. The town is called Wisdom Peak."

Mickey clenched his jaw, clearly perturbed by the sheriff's cheekiness. "I'm going to enjoy killing you."

Wiz and Mickey were on the outskirts of the town within moments. A handful of the townspeople stood by, watching from a safe distance.

Mickey was ecstatic to finally get to shoot something, but also curious. The boy agreed to a duel, but still didn't bother to arm himself. He also had an eerie calm and confidence about him that only pissed Mickey off even more.

"Twenty paces and I will only use one shot," Mickey said.

"Fine by me," Wiz replied as they took their positions and turned away from one another.

Mickey "Grim Gun" McGraw was by no means an honorable man, but when it came to his reputation as the best gunslinger to ever live, he refused to give anyone reason to doubt the fairness of his duels. The boy obviously had some trick up his sleeve and he refused to use a gun by his own choice, so Mickey had no qualms about shooting him even if he wasn't armed. He would give the boy his twenty paces. The little negro sheriff would need to appreciate these last few moments of life...

Eighteen...

Mickey wondered if the boy ever got to know the touch of a woman. He figured after he was done with the sheriff, he would get a room in town and invite the pretty girl from the bar over...

Nineteen...

Mickey also made a mental note to kill that barkeep. He didn't like the man's tone when he spoke or the look of defiance in his eyes. The guy didn't even show any respect when he told him his name.

TWENTY!

Mickey spun on his heels, pulling a single revolver from his hip, training his weapon on the back of his opponent's head before he could fully complete his own turn, and squeezing off one shot.

BANG!

Mickey grinned expecting the blood spatter and the final spasm of the body before it hit the ground... But neither came.

"I guess your reputation was all hot air, friend," the cheeky sheriff taunted as he turned and smiled politely at Mickey.

The onlookers laughed, but Mickey was fuming. Something was wrong here.

Mickey fired two more shots, one for the head and one aimed for the chest. This time he saw the disturbance in the sand as both bullets dropped several feet away from the sheriff and landed harmlessly on the ground.

"I think there might be something wrong with your weapons," the boy said. "I'll just come to you if it makes your aim easier."

There came more laughter from the onlookers as the sheriff smoothly strolled toward Mickey.

Mickey pulled his second revolver as he rushed toward Wiz, firing both weapons until they were emptied. Every bullet stopped short of Wiz, as if some invisible barrier protected him.

Mickey roared in outrage, but never slowed his charge. "This is some stupid trick! You tampered with my guns!"

Wiz only shook his head, but he looked pityingly at Mickey now.

With only a few more steps between them, Mickey then dropped both shooters and drew his knife, raising it over his head to strike down at Wiz's heart. The sheriff didn't bother to raise a hand to defend himself, but continued to move forward casually the whole time Mickey advanced on him with his hands at his side. And just when the knife came within an inch of Wiz's person, the world seemed to stop.

Mickey was in mid-step and his arm in full swing when his body suddenly tensed, gripped by some massive unseen force. His wrist snapped backward, and each finger on his knife-wielding hand twisted into an unnatural position as every bone snapped until he finally released the weapon. The knife fell from his grasp, but instead of hitting the ground, it hovered in the air with the blade turned toward Mickey's heart.

"Yield, sir," Wiz said.

"Never," Mickey growled, struggling against the mysterious power holding him in place, trying to conceal his fear. "I will kill every person in your little town to keep anyone from ever speakin' of this, you stupid, little ni—"

CRUNCH!

Mickey suddenly collapsed to the ground, no longer suspended by the odd power and now dead at the feet of Sheriff Wiz Armstrong.

His knife fell next to him. The blade was still clean.

By merely concentrating on the sand, Wiz buried Mickey's body in the very spot he'd died within the hour. To any casual observer, it would've appeared as if the earth simply opened its maw to swallow the corpse and snapped its jaws shut to hide the evidence six feet below under the pounds of grit. There was no need to deliver such a despicable human to the undertaker's parlor to be prepared for proper burial. No one would grieve him.

The story would be told that Mickey simply died of a fatal wound to his pride when he failed to kill the young sheriff with one shot as he'd done to so many men before. Either that, or his body gave in to some kind of infection, which was very common in these parts. The truth of the matter was that he died from the blunt force that imploded his chest and crushed his heart—blunt force caused by something unseen and unfathomable to most people in these times. No one needed to know the truth and no one would probably care too much that the Grim Gun was dead. The world was better for it. And besides, both cruel and kind men were taken by the desert every day.

Wiz returned to Winchester's saloon shortly after the duel. No one in the Winchester family bothered to observe the contest.

"We don't need to observe violence," Wesley simply said. "We just need the means to protect ourselves."

"If by 'the means to protect yourself', Wes, you mean guns, I think you would also be contributing to the town's problems," Wiz said, casually leaning on the bar. "When I arrived here, some of your regulars were toting guns and threatening each other on the suspicion of card cheats. But you've got me now. And this town is isolated enough that guys like Mickey McGraw are few and far between to be a certifiable threat to our peace to justify the need for guns in our society."

"But guys like Mickey McGraw will always exist, even after the Grim Reaper is finished with him, Wiz,"

Wesley replied. "And you've got great powers, but being everywhere ain't one of them."

"True..." Wiz said. "However, as long as we band together as a community, I'll at least have eyes and ears everywhere."

"Well, let's hope in the next incident like that you won't have this town's blood everywhere too, *Mr. Savior of Wisdom Peak.*"

Wiz laughed at the last statement, though he hated it when someone referred to him in that way. "I am no savior. Just a sheriff who wants to protect everyone in this town to the best of his *supernatural* ability."

It was Wesley's turn to chuckle. "You are indeed a gift, sir. But we have to wonder how long it can keep on giving. We're all human. We all have our limits. I hope I would never have to see the day my Esther would have to stitch you together or the undertaker would have to get you. I would hope you find something greater for yourself and your talents before that day comes..."

Wiz sighed. "Anything I could help you and Whitney with around here?"

"No," Wes said. "You've already helped plenty today."

The crowd of patrons began to come in waves to the saloon. Wiz enjoyed talking to Wes and Whitney, but he didn't care much to be around large groups. He often wondered if the small, tightknit community was part of the appeal for an introvert like himself to settle in the small town. He also sometimes wondered if he was meant to do more in the world beyond the limits of Wisdom Peak.

Wiz eventually left Wesley's establishment to return to his own office. Besides being his home and workplace, this was his quiet place. The jail had remained empty for several months now. Since he became the upholder of the law in Wisdom Peak, the only use for the jail was to hold the occasional belligerent drunk until they sobered up. It really was a peaceful and productive town. Whether by the strength of virtue in the people themselves or by their fear of the power Wiz wielded, which had been instilled in all of them since the day he arrived, it mattered not.

Wiz settled into his desk chair and removed the badge on his chest. He turned it over in his hands, staring at it pensively. He never had the chance to get to know the man who wore it before him.

Wiz never knew his mother or father either. He was told by his uncle, her own brother, his mother died of illness less than two years after Wiz's birth and no one ever met his father. Wiz's powers developed shortly after he was taken into his uncle's care, but he couldn't remember what happened that day either.

The most important day Wiz did remember was the day he came to Wisdom Peak. So many things happened in such a short time. It was several years ago, early spring when Wiz arrived to town near high noon while accompanying the man and woman he'd known as his Uncle Jean and Aunt Laverne. They raised Wiz, taught him how to talk, read and write, among other things. It was their guidance that gave him the sense of justice and every other virtue he lived by today.

"A man's words and actions show his character, but his character and principles reveal his soul," Jean would say.

"You can always offer mercy to someone who is despicable and kindness to someone who is disrespectful, but you cannot be a savior to someone who is incorrigibly wicked," Laverne once said.

They were kind, God-fearing people who despised guns, but the day they stopped in Wisdom Peak to buy supplies and rest, the very town that bore his own namesake, was the day they would be called to meet their Maker. Coincidentally, they told him Wisdom Peak was the same town his mother wanted to visit with them before she passed away and she chose his name for that reason.

The townspeople were kind enough, but there was some obvious discomfort among them to see the Black couple with the teenage boy. Of all the people here, the Winchester family was the most hospitable and genuine. Wiz especially took a liking to them and his uncle told him that people like them were few and far in this world. Wiz knew what he meant, but he didn't know he would encounter such an extreme opposite to these people in the same day.

The bandits came at sundown. Apparently one of their own had been captured for shooting a man upon entering town only a day before the Armstrong family's arrival. There were at least a score of them, all riding on horseback and armed with guns. They smashed bottles of oil and set fire to several buildings around the township, laying siege primarily to the jailhouse, and terrorizing the townsfolk. Of course, with their homes threatened, the people fought back. Gunfire was heard in every direction. It was a battlefield.

Wiz remembered seeing young Whitney Winchester, just shy of her twelfth birthday, screaming as a burning piece of debris fell towards her from above and two men on horses raced past, nearly trampling her. Her parents were trapped inside their home due to a collapsed roof and she was in the path of death.

Wiz remembered his uncle screaming in his ear, telling him not to draw attention to himself, not to be a hero. Keeping a low profile with White folks was always Uncle Jean's directive. However, in this moment, Wiz just reacted. With a single burst of telekinetic power, Wiz flung the burning debris from over Whitney's head and threw both men and horses into the air and over the buildings. He watched them fall, screaming in anguish as they landed in the remains of a nearby burning building. One of the horses landed safely, at least, falling just outside of the building and managing to get back up and run away.

Whitney was still screaming, but she was safe in the moment, until three more of the marauders appeared. Wiz tried to run over to the girl, but suddenly felt someone tackle him from behind and he fell to the ground just as he heard two gunshots.

Wiz turned to find the bleeding body of his Uncle Jean on top of him. Jean had been shot in the neck and chest, apparently hit by shots meant for Wiz. Wiz looked around to find his aunt, but she was nowhere in sight. He screamed for help, though some part of him knew none would come. He looked back to where Whitney was, just in time to see her father step outside of the building she stood in front of and pull her to safety before raising his own rifle and dispatching the approaching group of bandits.

Wesley Winchester noticed Wiz in the street, cradling his uncle. Once Whitney was safely inside, Mr. Winchester rushed over to help Wiz drag Jean to safety, assuring him that his wife, Esther, a skilled medicine woman, would do everything she could to save him. That was enough for Wiz. He couldn't hide anymore. There was a chance his aunt was still alive and he was compelled to do everything in his power to keep it that way.

Wiz had little practice with his abilities, but something in the back of his mind guided him, making the use of his power feel as natural as walking. He found another pair of pillagers who he immediately flung into a pile of debris, impaling them both on the large splinters of a damaged structure. Without hesitation, Wiz launched himself into the air, flying high above the buildings, hoping he could get a glimpse of his aunt or their horses somewhere below. However, he had no such luck. The smoke from the burning buildings was rising and obscuring his sight of everything below. Wiz lowered himself back to the ground, but he continued to use his power to levitate only a few feet from the ground now.

Moving down the street, he encountered another marauder assaulting a young woman. Wiz didn't bother to slow down as he launched the man across the ground into a nearby stable, startling the horses who promptly trampled the man to death. The young woman looked around in confusion, but cowered briefly when she laid eyes on the young man who briskly floated past her.

Wiz crushed, impaled, and smashed several more men that night before the violence came to an end. This was the first time he used his powers to kill and he killed far more people than any person with a gun in Wisdom Peak that night. When the dust cleared, all of the bandits were dead and the bodies of at least twelve citizens of Wisdom Peak, including two children and the sheriff, were found. The most devastating discovery was the corpse of Laverne. A single bullet wound was in her back and she'd been severely burned and cut.

Wiz's last disappointment was at the remains of the Winchester home. His uncle succumbed to his wounds shortly after saving Wiz's life. Esther Winchester did all that she could, but fate had greater use for Jean's life.

Wiz did not know where to go or what to do. He remained in the town, grieving the loss of the only family he knew and using his abilities to help the people rebuild their homes and businesses. They were in awe of this young Black man with this tremendous power that neither he nor they could understand, but they were grateful for his assistance. Wiz did not learn until later that the people who witnessed him flying over the town thought they were observing an angel descending on Wisdom Peak in its greatest time of need.

As talks of Wiz's feats spread across and beyond the town over the following weeks, the people of Wisdom Peak decided to name him as sheriff. Their respect for him grew so much they allowed him to propose new laws to protect them as he saw fit. The first of these would be the abolition of guns from the town.

It only took about two weeks following the death of Mickey McGraw before three new strangers arrived to town on horses. None of them carried guns as far as anyone could tell, but Wesley Winchester was the first to notice something eerie and menacing about this trio when they entered his saloon.

The one who strode in ahead of the other two was a tall, broad-shouldered man with olive skin and dark eyes and dark hair tied back into a queue. He flashed a smile at Whitney and gave a quick nod toward some of the other patrons who could not help but glance at the imposing figure as he made his way toward the bar. The man was relatively well-dressed, but still coated with the dust from days of riding on horseback across the desert. He didn't seem like the type to be accustomed to riding in carriages anyway.

The tall man sat himself down and gave a quick nod to Wesley. "Barkeep, could I get some water for myself, my friends and our horses as well? Your trough outside looks a bit low."

Wesley nodded and noted the man's Spanish accent confirming his suspicions, though his dress style was more typical of the Native American people he'd encountered in his years. The man had a casual air about him, but something beneath it seemed off to Wesley.

The man's two companions joined him at the bar. One was a rather homely man with pale skin, a broad nose and lips, a balding scalp, and shifty blue eyes. In stark contrast to this one, the third member of their group, a striking, slender woman dressed in similar attire to her male counterparts, commanded the attention of every person in the bar just as the taller man did. She had fiery red hair, bright green eyes, and a distinct scar across her forehead that appeared to Wesley as if it had been made by a dulled knife.

Wesley caught himself before his eyes lingered too long on the woman whose rare beauty was only tainted by the sullen expression worn on her face rather than the scar. He gestured to Whitney from across the room.

"Dear, could you replenish the water outside?" Wesley asked as he moved to retrieve glasses for the guests.

"Oh, that's your daughter?" the homely man said with an odd smirk as Wesley returned with the filled cups. "Good for you. But you should probably train her better in how she judges strangers who patronize your establishment."

"Excuse me?" Wesley said pushing the cups to the new guests, not hiding the defensiveness in his voice. Whitney was simply standing by the door when the trio entered, but she made no gestures or even spoke to them, however the man's voice sounded threatening.

"I mean no harm, sir," the pale man said, taking a swig from his cup. "I'm simply acknowledging that she seemed to pass some judgement upon viewing us."

"She didn't speak a word to you, sir," Wesley rebutted.

"No, but there are more than words to convey feelings," the man said, his eyes darting from his companions to Wesley. "Kind of like the expression on your face upon viewing my more lovely companion, Sienna, here."

"Stop, Cal," the red-haired woman demanded after finishing the last of her beverage. "You're unnerving the host and making enemies for us before we can develop proper *friendships.*"

She made eye contact with Wesley as she spoke the last word and forced a smile. For a moment, Wesley thought he glimpsed something that resembled a hideous, horned demon with melted flesh beneath her visage. He felt himself recoil and upon seeing his reaction, the woman's tight smile spread into a genuine grin.

"I said I meant no harm," Cal said, casting glances over his shoulder, seemingly trying to keep an eye on every person within the saloon. "A dignified married man probably should avoid lusting after young women, just as much as a young woman shouldn't judge strangers so harshly is all I was suggesting."

"Never mind him, barkeep," the Mestizo man said pulling a parchment from the inside of his vest. "He's a bit strange, I know, but I assure you, he's harmless. Thank you for the drink. Could you tell us if you've seen this man, the one they call the 'Grim Gun'?"

The leader unfolded the paper to reveal a drawing of Mickey McGraw's face.

"Yes, as a matter of fact, I have," Wesley said. "He came through here some weeks ago, making trouble. Threatened some people, had it out with the sheriff, and ended up buried just outside of town. I'd advise you folks not to follow in his footsteps."

The tanned man's dark eyes narrowed. He turned to the pale man who looked up sheepishly at him and nodded as if affirming something unspoken between them. The dark eyes then set back on Wesley. Even in the heat of the summer, Wesley had never felt the air in the room suddenly warm as it did now.

"You say the sheriff took the Grim Gun out?" the man's face seemed to grow darker and his tone became more aggressive as he stood from his barstool.

"He ain't no ordinary sheriff, Deacon," the pale man said, his eyes fixed on Wesley. "He's one of us…"

At that, Wesley's eyes widened and the tanned man, Deacon, seemed to settle down, smirking slightly.

"*Really now?*" Deacon said. "Where can I find the sheriff?"

As if he was summoned by the simple mentioning of his title, Wiz entered the saloon. He greeted the other patrons as he entered, but Wesley noticed the sheriff's attention almost instantly shifted to the three strangers at the bar. Just as Wesley looked up at the sheriff approaching, the three strangers seemed to turn to observe him as well, all standing up to get a better look, or possibly to prepare for whatever was to come next.

"That there is our sheriff, Wisdom Armstrong," Wesley said, feeling slightly relieved.

Wiz tilted the brim of his hat to the group as he got to the bar and leaned on the counter, casting a quick glance at each of them, sizing them up. Like every other man, his eyes lingered longer on the woman.

"Hello, friends," Wiz said addressing the group. "As Mr. Winchester said, I'm Sheriff Wisdom Armstrong. Just noticed the three of you here and wanted to give you a proper welcome to Wisdom Peak. While you're staying, I have to ask that the three of you leave your guns with me. By law, those weapons are not permitted here."

Just as Wiz finished his sentence, there was a sudden glimmer. Wesley then noticed it. Each of the three had a gun on their hip, the woman had two. Some of the other men nearby seemed to gasp noticing the sudden appearance of the weapons.

"He saw through my illusion," the redhead said, inclining her head. "He's definitely one of us."

The tall man rose fully to his feet, smirking. He extended a hand. "A pleasure, Sheriff. We were just about to come looking for you."

Wiz cocked his head to one side and raised an eyebrow, briefly glancing toward Wesley suspiciously, but shaking the tanned man's hand all the same. "And why is that?"

"I wanted to meet the man who took my revenge from me," the taller man replied. "But more importantly, I was interested in meeting another *gifted* brother." This the man said with the most sincere smile he'd given since his arrival.

Chapter 4: The Four Revenants

"My name is Deacon," the tall man said. "Deacon Brand. The lady is Sienna Pearce. The other gentleman here is Calum Borman. We call him Cal for short."

Cal and Sienna nodded as Deacon introduced them.

"Nice to meet you," Wiz said. "You can refer to me as sheriff or just Wiz, whichever you prefer, but again, I insist you surrender your weapons before we offer any further hospitality. One at a time and slowly... *Please.*"

"Oh, of course," Deacon said, slowly undoing the holster on his belt to gently hand his gun to Wiz first. "I assume there is no need for us to protect ourselves from any of the good people in this town?"

Wiz set the gun on the counter. "You have my word."

Sienna pulled both of her weapons and sarcastically bowed as she offered them to Wiz as if presenting a tribute. "Take good care of them and me, little lawman," she said with a wink.

Cal shuffled toward Wiz, his eyes darting around the saloon. Wiz tensed slightly, unsure of what to expect from this one. Cal exchanged a look with Deacon before finally handing his gun over.

"Thank you all for your compliance," Wiz said to the trio.

"Sure thing," Deacon said. "Now, is there some place we can speak privately? Being unarmed around crowds makes my friends a bit nervous, as you can see."

"We can head over to my office," Wiz said. Turning to Wesley, he added, "Can I get a box to carry these guns in?"

Wesley understood. Wiz was trying to conceal his own abilities, at least for now.

Wiz led the group a short ways through the town. The three newcomers remained silent, apparently observing their surroundings.

Upon arriving at the sheriff's office, a lovely middle-aged woman with a strong resemblance to the barkeeper's daughter, including the bright green eyes and blonde hair, stepped out of the building. She smiled brightly upon seeing Wiz.

"Hi, dear!" she said. "I was just looking for you. I left you some meat, cheese, milk and moonshine at your station."

"I appreciate it, Mrs. Winchester," Wiz said gently taking both of her hands in one of his and tucking the box he carried under one arm. "You know you don't need to bring me the alcohol though. I can't stand the stuff and it does nothing good for anybody."

"I know, but it is just the regular offering from Wesley," she said, shrugging. She then looked over at the group behind Wiz. "Apologies to your guests.

If either of you requires any medical attention, please come to see me."

Wiz turned to the band of outsiders. "Mrs. Winchester is—"

"Esther Winchester, the medicine woman and the barkeeper's wife," Calum said, staring through the woman. "Mother of the pretty little waitress."

Wiz noticed Mrs. Winchester shift uncomfortably. She was a very friendly and personable woman, and there were few people if any she'd ever met who made her visibly uncomfortable.

"Yes, I am," Mrs. Winchester said, still holding a polite smile. Addressing Wiz, she said, "Well, it is a slow day in my practice, but you are clearly busy, so I will leave you to your meeting and go visit my husband. Farewell and y'all enjoy your stay!"

Mrs. Winchester briskly walked away as Wiz brought the trio into his office.

Deacon and the others seated themselves on a long wooden bench opposite of the only desk in the whole building. The furnishings in the building were very limited. With the exception of the small wood desk and the bench, there was a single bed beside the desk that had been recently slept in and a few small cots within the jail cell along the wall farthest from the entrance.

Wiz seated himself in the single chair behind the desk, placing the box containing the group's weapons beneath the table. The only thing on top of the table was the basket of goods left by Mrs. Winchester and an open Bible.

"Welcome to my home and office, lady and gentlemen," Wiz said, gesturing around the room. "So, what is your business here and what would you like to discuss?"

"You seem to have a nice setup here," Deacon said, smirking again. "Young, colored man, respected by the folks here, holding the law in his hands and even receiving offerings from them. You must not have a care in the world, huh?"

"I have plenty of cares," Wiz replied. "My care is for the folks here. And I have concerns when strangers come to my town."

"*Your town?*" Deacon echoed, his mouth stretching into a grin as he leaned forward. "Mmm... Must be nice! I've never had a town... Or a real home, for that matter. Truthfully, maybe I just never wanted it. I am blessed to have a family though. These two here are all that's left of it."

Wiz simply raised an eyebrow.

"That egotistical piece of scum McGraw murdered a member of our family when we crossed paths with him about a month ago," Deacon continued. "We embarrassed him, so he wanted to make a point by taking the life of one of ours. His bullet was meant for me. The man he killed, Ash, could see flashes of the future. He saved my life by pushing me out of the way. Unfortunately, as you probably already know, our abilities don't work on other gifted people. Ash couldn't see my future and he couldn't react fast enough to save his own. McGraw evaded us, but I take some pleasure in knowing someone like us took him out of this world.”

“What makes you think I’m like you?” Wiz asked trying to conceal any emotion from his face.

“I read the barkeeper’s mind,” Cal interjected. “When he thought of you, his memories showed what you could do. You move things with your mind. He is afraid of you, but he does seem to genuinely care for you and respect you, too. Even though he seems to take some privileges over your law. Also, I cannot read your mind.”

Wiz was unsure what he meant by that last part about Wesley taking “privileges” and he felt moved to know Wesley cared for him. The Winchester’s had been the closest thing to family for him since the loss of his aunt and uncle. But he was most intrigued by this group now.

“You also saw through my glamor,” Sienna said with the slightest hint of a smile on her lips. “I keep our weapons hidden to give us the element of surprise, but you were the only one in this town who could see through my charm."

"So, you know what I can do and you know what I did to Mickey McGraw," Wiz said. "So, what do you want from me?"

Deacon stood up and snapped his fingers. Flames instantly ignited on his fingertips. The fire swirled and slid from his fingers, into the palm of his hand. He closed his hand and the flame vanished. He extended his open palm toward Wiz to show there were no burns.

"We want you to join our family," Deacon said. "You could take Ash's place with us as a member of the Four Revenants. That's what we call ourselves because each of us has died to something only to return with greater power. With these *gifts* we have now, we are like walking spirits on earth with abilities that make us more than what we once were. You must have experienced some type of death in your life as well to have the power you possess, right? Probably your parents?"

Wiz's mind immediately went to his Uncle Jean and Aunt Laverne. Also, the mother he never knew. "Yeah, I have," he said staring off, forgetting his surroundings for a moment.

Deacon strode over to the desk and extended his hand. Wiz didn't know if he was going to blast fire into his face or if that was even a possibility based on what they'd already said. He quickly stood up, ready to defend himself, but Deacon kept his hand extended in a gesture of acceptance.

"Will you join us, brother?"

Chapter 5: The Gifted

"What does joining you mean exactly?" Wiz asked.

"It means you share what you have with us, and we do the same," Deacon said, snatching a piece of cheese from the Winchesters' basket and taking a bite, chewing while he continued. "Your power is our power and ours is yours. We look out for each other. We all move together. If you join us, we can have a bigger town together. Or, we could stay here and make something more of this place."

Wiz noticed there was a slight change in Deacon's tone with that last statement.

"I'll need some time to think about it," Wiz replied, moving the basket away from Deacon's reach, but taking the bottle of moonshine out and pushing it toward him. "You're welcome to the drink, though. There is also an inn near the saloon if you need a place to rest."

"Sure," Deacon said, accepting the bottle. "I guess we should get comfortable with each other first before any big decisions are made. We could give it a few days. Perhaps you could show us around a bit?"

"As you could imagine, as sheriff, I'm a busy man, but you're welcome to explore the town on your own so long as you don't stir up any trouble," Wiz replied. "I can meet with you at the saloon or here later in day."

Deacon dropped his hand, but continued to smile. "Fine. See you soon then, brother. We'll be out and about, getting a feel for the locals then."

Deacon opened the bottle of moonshine, taking a swig as he strode out of the sheriff's office. Sienna gave Wiz a quick wink before turning to follow Deacon and Cal outside.

Despite the beauty of the redhead, Wiz felt something unsettling about her flirtation. There was something behind all of the Revenants' eyes that seemed sinister. Was what Deacon said about each

of them dying to something to gain their power true?
Was he, like them, a spirit walking the earth? Is that
what the people of Wisdom Peak saw and feared in
him?

Wiz ventured through the town, patrolling the area,
though his mind was still elsewhere. Despite the
presence of Deacon's group, there was still a sense of
normalcy. Nadine, a sultry woman of the night, was
busy chatting up her next customer. In such a small
town, Wiz easily recognized the john, but chose to
mind his own business. Barry, the town's biggest
drunk, was getting his afternoon nap under a nearby
trough outside of his neighbor's home. Jonah, an
elderly cardsharp, was collecting debt owed from the
last week, most likely planning to wager his earnings
in another game at the saloon later tonight.

Per his routine, the last stop on Wiz's patrol was the
Winchester saloon. He'd encountered none of the
Revenants and began to wonder if they'd either
holed up in the local inn or decided it best to leave

town. Wiz knew the latter was not very likely, but he felt a sense of dread nonetheless when his eyes met with Deacon's upon entering the pub.

Deacon sat alone at a table near the center of the drinkery, the bottle of moonshine he'd taken from Wiz's office in his hand, now nearly empty. Deacon smiled, lifting the bottle and gesturing for Wiz to join him.

Wiz cast a glance to the bar as he made his way over to the table, noting neither Wesley or Whitney were anywhere in sight. *Odd.* Some of the regular patrons were present, but they were all seated closer to the walls of the establishment, apparently keeping their distance from the intimidating stranger.

Wiz took a seat at the round table to Deacon's left rather than directly across from him. He wanted to position his body to ensure he'd have a clear view of the main door in case Deacon's two companions should show up.

"You're a Bible-reading man, right?" Deacon asked, leaning uncomfortably close to Wiz's face. "One of my favorite Bible stories growing up was about that boy Samson, who was blessed with godly strength. His power may have been from God, but he could and would do everything he wanted as a kind of god among men. Even that broad, Deborah, who had the power of prophecy was gifted with powers more like our own. The way I see it, people like us are like them. We are gifted with power from the heavens to rule and do as we please on earth. I think in my younger days, I've lit a few coyote tails on fire before to see if I could burn a whole town down like Samson did with the foxes."

"I really think you're missing the point of those Old Testament stories, friend," Wiz said, looking askance at the other man.

"Well, I had the stories read to me growing up," Deacon admitted with a shrug. "I was never one for interpreting them. But I'm not wrong, am I? Here you are ruling your own little colony here with an iron fist. You've taken away the people's ability to defend themselves by outlawing guns and made yourself their sole means of protection. What would you call that?"

"A safety precaution," Wiz replied flatly.

Deacon laughed, slapping his knee. "Well, when you've got powers beyond a regular man, you can cast precaution to the wind. However, I'm not mad at a man who makes his own law."

"Laws are intended to save lives," Wiz said. "That's my only intention. You talk a lot about power, but even in Samson's story, he had a weakness and he died like any other man would. And Deborah used her power to serve others—"

"Well, that Samson died on his own terms, I believe," Deacon said. "And the true question is, what do the people here need to be saved from? It's your law. So, you're their one and only savior here?"

"I'm just the sheriff."

"Right, well people always find a way to destroy themselves, don't they? Maybe they need someone with powers like you to keep them in line... Just for their own good, right? Do you even think someone who looks like you or me would ever truly be accepted as sheriff or in any position of authority, if not for our power? Considering the lack of color in this town, I think you've got more fear than respect going for you."

Wiz could not come up with a response to that.

"You're a king here," Deacon said. "I assumed from our earlier exchange you're an orphan, too, like me. Like Cal. Like Sienna. We all gained power through pain. That is something great to be honored. We should be honored as well for what we came from and what we were made to do here on earth."

"You're all orphans?" Wiz asked.

"Yeah... I think it's something we are born with and tragedy is what triggers us to become who we are. I watched my own mother get abused and then killed by wealthy White men... The moment the light left her eyes was the moment the fire exploded from every part of me. I turned every one of them to ash with a thought. Sienna also spent her whole life trying to protect herself from lustful, wicked men, hiding behind her illusions ever since her own abusive father killed her mom and put that nasty scar across her beautiful face. She drove him mad until he wandered into the desert and nature had its way with him. Calum's own parents abandoned him when he was a toddler. He was taken in and grew up trying to find work where he could, trying to find people who would value him, but the world is unkind if you don't look a certain way. Constant mistreatment and witnessing violence awakened his power and he realized what people really thought of him and each other. He gave up on earning acceptance from people once he could hear their inner voices and understood their self-loathing would prevent them from ever being accepting or happy with themselves, let alone him. Even Ash witnessed a betrayal his family never saw coming when his own uncle murdered his father to steal an heirloom and some money. Eventually, we found each other."

"Sounds like a rough existence," Wiz said, lowering his eyes. "I guess when you put it that way, it was the wickedness of the world that brought us all here together, too. Not just the actions of Mickey McGraw, but everything. Maybe there is a divine plan in there somewhere."

Deacon finished the last of the moonshine and grinned. "Yep! Brought together as if it were by God's own hands, crafting some divine joke about a bunch of powered folks meeting in a bar or something. It's a definite maybe, brother. I think there is something that speaks to me every time I use my power. It is a quiet voice, so the words are unclear, but I believe it to be the voice of God."

"And if you stopped to listen, what do you believe He would tell you to do?" Wiz asked, completely letting his guard down now.

Deacon laughed, smacking the palm of his hand on the tabletop. "I think you missed my point, brother. God may have made me and given me power and purpose, but I'm not interested in the direction someone else tries to push me in or following some plan I had no part in designing. I'm going to use my power, my own control and will, to be a head and never a tail. You understand me?"

Wiz did understand. He had never heard the voice clearly himself, but there was always a feeling, a presence that touched him when he used his abilities. The first time he recognized it, it scared him, but since then he grew comfortable. Maybe he wasn't trying to listen either.

"Sure, you have a choice in using your gift, but what if you're not connecting that power to your purpose?" Wiz said, suddenly realizing he was thinking out loud to himself and to the man before him. "What if you're doing everything all wrong and not living your life to the fullest because you aren't seeking direction? We were all given power and brought together for some reason, but what if you're not in the right place, with the right people, or doing the right thing that would make your life greater?"

"Well, that is *my choice*," Deacon said, staring Wiz in the eye with a new seriousness. "Everything me and my people went through, was in *His* plan, and so

I have no interest in what He has to say. I live every moment with intentions to be great, never to be a follower or victim again. The places I've been, people I've befriended or killed, and every action I've taken is my choice and I own it. You have a choice to make, too. You can consider the what ifs, but whether you seek and go with some divine plan or move on your own terms, whether you regret or relish your decision, every move is yours. Whether you accept or refuse our offer, you should be prepared to live and die with that choice."

Deacon pounded the table to emphasize the words of that last sentence. The other patrons of the bar were busying themselves with their own affairs and individual conversations, but went silent and turned their attention to the two young men then. Wiz did not flinch, but he detected an underlying threat in Deacon's words, and based on his demeanor, it wasn't just the moonshine talking.

Deacon rose from the table, just swaying ever so slightly. "I will be at the little inn near the medicine woman's place if you want to talk about the future."

"Yeah, I will be in touch," Wiz said. His fingers twitched as he contemplated making his move in that moment...

Deacon strutted toward the door, but paused before exiting. He turned to look over his shoulder at Wiz. "Speaking of the medicine woman, Cal was right about her husband, the barkeep. He has been defying your law. He's been keeping a cache of guns in a secret room here. As a show of good faith to you, I forced him to show me where the room was and melted the weapons down. Left the gunpowder though. It could be useful for something... Don't worry. I left him in one piece so you could personally deal with him your way. I only burned him a little, but with a bit of concentration I could've roasted him better than a pig on a spit."

With that, Deacon casually strode outside, chuckling to himself.

Wiz only stared off blankly towards the bar. His mind now reeling. His anger now seething.

Wiz lost all sense of time. After Deacon's departing words, he did not know how long he'd been sitting at the table before Whitney burst through the saloon doors with tears streaming down her face.

"Wiz! My daddy's been attacked! I found him behind this place not too long ago, bloodied and burned! He's alive and my ma's treating him, but I think—"

"Did you know?" Wiz asked standing up and walking past Whitney to go outside.

"Know what?" Whitney asked, her voice lowered from her previous shrill tone.

Wiz walked briskly down the path through town toward the Winchester family's home, staring ahead as if he were in a trance. "Did you know your father was secretly storing weapons?" he quietly asked.

Whitney hesitated and seemed to stop following Wiz momentarily before answering. "Yes."

Wiz spun on his heel to face her. His face was like stone, but his voice cracked from the strain of holding back his frustration and pain, but he managed to growl one word through gritted teeth. "Why?"

"Because, like he explained to me, he is a man with people he loves and things he must protect, and as a man, he could not rely on someone else's power to do that for him." Whitney said, her voice surprisingly calm despite the fresh tears running down her cheeks.

Wiz could tell that she could recognize his own pain from their betrayal. She cried now for him, not their own exposure. His expression softened, but he remained silent.

"You have to understand what he did was not about you and he did not do it to hurt you," Whitney said through her sobs. "Our family loves you more than you know."

Wiz turned back to continue to his destination. He could see the truth in her eyes, but Wesley was still on his mind. "I understand... But I need to hear everything from him before I make a decision."

Whitney walked behind Wiz in silence until they arrived at the door. Wiz paused briefly to be respectful and allow Whitney to open the door for him and usher him inside. He made his way to Wesley's bedroom in silence, quietly walking in to find the man lying in bed atop the covers with his wife seated in a chair at his side. Wesley's right forearm and right thigh were covered in wet rags and his face was heavily bruised.

Esther rose from the chair, opening her mouth to defend her husband, but Wesley quickly spoke up.

"It's okay, Esther," he said. "Please leave me and Wiz the room. You've done more than enough, sweetheart."

Esther silently nodded. She rose from her seat and dipped her head down as she briskly walked past Wiz, avoiding his eyes, her hands balled into fists. Whitney stood in the doorway and followed her mother as she rounded the corner to go to the family room.

Once they were alone, Wesley broke the silence first. "I guess I deserved this, huh? Gun or no gun, I'm lucky to be alive, being an ordinary man against someone with extraordinary power similar to your own."

"Do you think maybe if you had the option to use the guns you hid, if given the choice to fight back on your own terms, you would be in better condition?" Wiz asked.

"I believe what I said!" Wesley insisted. "I hid guns for several people in this town in the event one day we would need to defend ourselves, whether it be with you or against you. That's the whole truth. I hid something from you, and I was punished for my deceit... There is no getting around that. I couldn't hide my thoughts and I couldn't fight a man like that on my own. He even allowed me to pick up my own guns, dared me to use it against him, and I froze when I saw fire summoned to his fingertips. He is flesh... But I felt like I was facing something inhuman... Something unconquerable."

"I think even Deacon would agree with you on the thought of him being something other than human..." Wiz said dryly.

There was an awkward moment of silence while the two men's eyes roamed the room as if they were both searching for their next words. Then Wes said, "So, what will you do with me then, Sheriff Armstrong?"

Wiz sighed. "I think I can decide that once I've dealt with the greater matter at hand. Deacon's gang... they want me to join them. Either I leave with them or they will stay here. Either way, I don't have the power to see the future, but I don't see things ending well for this town. Whether they go now or stay and bleed it dry, they will definitely leave it in ruins."

Wes sat up straighter in bed, nodding and finally meeting Wiz's eyes. "So, how do you propose we stop them?"

Wiz couldn't help but smile as he cocked his head and raised an eyebrow at the older man. " *We?* You're barely fit enough to wrestle with tumbleweed, old man."

Wes grinned back, waving his good arm with a tight fist. "I'm tougher than I look and I owe that fire-starting hell spawn some payback. Plus, I've got to protect my girls... even if I can't save myself..."

"Even if you can't save yourself, I'll save you," Wiz said confidently. "I'm upset by what you've done, but I was taught by my aunt and uncle that you have to be quick and intentional with forgiveness, especially with those you consider family. Outsiders harming the people of this town in is a greater offense than anything you've done. And no transgression by you could undo all the good you Winchesters have done for me."

Wes nodded, the corners of his mouth twitched and his lower eyelids moistened. A lump suddenly formed in his throat and something swelled in his chest. He turned his head for a moment to wipe his eyes on the back of his good arm and clear his throat, pushing the emotions away.

"So, again, how do you intend to stop them?" Wes asked turning back to Wiz once he composed himself. "There're three of them, one of you, and we now have no guns to help you."

"Actually, we've got *their* guns and other weapons, too," Wiz said. "You'll just need an opening to use them. So will I. Apparently, our powers don't work directly on each other, so I can't kill them like a normal group of gangsters. But they can't hurt me so easily either. Also, they don't seem to be aware of the one weakness I've avoided all of my life."

Now Wes raised an eyebrow and inclined his head. "You had a weakness all this time?"

"You never wondered why I never consumed spirits?" Wiz asked, smirking.

Wes shrugged. "I always thought it was just a point of pride or faith thing with you."

Wiz shook his head. "More like a protection thing. My power is derived from focusing my mind. If I can't focus, I'm powerless. A drunk mind is clouded and useless. We can use that against them."

Wes nodded. He swung his legs around to the edge of the bed and pushed himself up to stand. He held out his left hand to Wiz. "Thank you for trusting me with that. You have my complete trust now as well."

Wiz took Wes' hand in his own and shook it. "Good. I trust you can prepare the gunpowder you had stashed away. I don't expect you to sacrifice your life, but you may need to sacrifice your livelihood for us to win this coming fight, Mr. Winchester."

Wes hesitated for a moment, realizing what the sheriff was asking him to do. Esther and Whitney peeked around the corner, catching Wesley's eye and strengthening his resolve. "You got it, sheriff."

"Good," Wiz said. "You'll need to make sure the townsfolk stay clear of your place, but get the word out for them to arm themselves anyway they can so they are ready if things escalate. I will just need to deal with Cal first.”

Wiz turned to look back at the two women. His eyes suddenly brightened as a stroke of inspiration hit him. “We may all have a role to play. But you need to rest first, Wes.”

Chapter 7: Assassin and Defender

Two days later, the town was in disarray. Jonah was being savagely beaten by several other men who were screaming at him. "Cheater! Thief! That stranger told us you've been using dirty tricks to win our games! Now we see he was right! You had extra cards hidden up your sleeves and trousers every night."

With a single wave of one hand, Wiz used his abilities to force the group of assailants away from the older gentleman. With a stern look and a cock of his head, they immediately retreated from the scene. Wiz knew the men spoke of Cal, but he did not have time to verify with Jonah if the accusations against him were true. He had other matters to attend to.

Wiz only made it a short distance before he arrived at another unsettling scene. Nadine thrashed about wildly in the street, scratching at her own face and shrieking, "No! Get them off of me! They are burrowing into my face! Help me! Please!" Nothing that could be seen by others touched the woman, but she clawed at something nonetheless, creating long gashes in her once beautiful face. People looked on in concern, but they were clearly at a loss for what to do for her sudden fit of madness.

Miming a pincer with one hand, Wiz pinned her arms to her sides and levitated her over a nearby water trough, forcing her to look into her own reflection in the liquid surface so she could see for herself she was in no danger. Once she calmed down, Wiz took some of the water in his hands to gently wipe some of the blood from her brow to prevent it from running into her eyes. He instructed her to see Mrs. Winchester to be treated for the self-inflicted wounds. He wasn't sure how long the illusion planted in her mind would affect her or if it could return once she was out of his sight, but he prayed for her safety as he continued on his own way.

Barry seemed to be in his normal routine, sleeping near the saloon. Most likely waiting for Wes to return so he could get his next fill. Wes tapped the drunk with his foot and whispered sharply, "I know sober might be a new word for you, Barry, but I need you to take it home with you tonight. The bar will be closed for a special occasion, friend."

Deacon sat up and stretched, now rested from a brief nap. The bed in the quaint inn did not offer the best sleep he'd ever had, but he did sleep. And it definitely beat the comfort of the makeshift beds he and his crew had become accustomed to.

It was time he revisited his new brother. He'd given the young sheriff some time to consider his proposal, even avoiding the jailhouse or the bar since their last encounter the other day. He'd taken his time to study the other townsfolk and get the lay of the land. Wisdom Peak was certainly dull, but if he and his crew were to remain, Deacon had already resolved to bring a new spark to the place to liven things up. He'd encouraged Cal and Sienna to have their fun as well.

KNOCK. KNOCK. KNOCK.

Someone was at the door to his small quarters. Fortunately, for whoever the guest was, he was already fully clothed. Not that modesty was a concern for him.

He opened the door to find the pretty little barmaid in the hallway. He grinned. "To what do I owe this pleasure?"

Whitney trembled at the sight of the man, both fear and rage in her heart. She did her best to keep her voice steady. "The sh—sheriff is r-r-requesting to meet with you at the saloon, sir."

Deacon raised an eyebrow. "I just saw him there not too long ago. Why didn't he come himself?"

"He had another matter to attend to, but wanted me to let you know he would be along soon."

Deacon sighed, but then put on a quick smile. He pulled one of Whitney's tiny, pale, delicate hands into his own large, dark, weathered grip. "Fine then. I don't mind returning that way as long as you don't mind walking along with me."

Whitney managed to summon the courage to look him in the eye and nod, putting on her best fake smile she'd practiced using on so many patrons of her father's establishment.

Deacon pulled the door to the room closed behind him as he continued to eye the small girl, who still trembled and avoided looking at him for too long. "How is your daddy by the way?" he asked, a hint of amusement in his voice.

The girl suddenly straightened and her trembling ceased. She turned and looked up at Deacon with an intensity in her eyes he'd only seen in his own reflection and a smile and sudden calmness that even made him uneasy. "He is well, sir. He had an accident at the bar and burned himself, but he is recovering nicely. Thank you for asking."

Deacon knew she was feigning ignorance, but it didn't matter. He was liking her more every moment. He followed her to the bar in silence, still grinning and growing curious.

Sienna sat at the edge of a porch, toying with the broach she just recently obtained from the jealous harlot she'd come across. The woman looked at her with such envy when she passed, the look in her eye repulsed Sienna. It almost reminded her of the look of so many men who cursed or attempted to violate her. The woman in the streets would never offend anyone with that repulsive look again though. By now, with the illusion Sienna had placed in her mind, she would have clawed those wretched eyes out of her own skull. Sienna grinned to herself admiring the broach in her hands.

"Excuse me, ma'am?"

Sienna looked up to see the medicine woman smiling warmly down at her. Something about this woman's demeanor pissed her off, too. Her polite personality was uncommon, a quality only afforded to a woman who had been protected all her life.

"What do you want?" Sienna asked.

"I just wanted to pass along the sheriff's invitation to join him for drinks. If you'd like, I can accompany you to the saloon."

Sienna's grin broadened. So, the little lawman wanted to get to know her better after all. She dropped the broach and rose to her feet, brushing past the medicine woman to make her way to the drinkery.

Cal stood near an alley snickering to himself as the chaos nearby unfolded. The people of the small town were so close, they probably had a deep trust for one another. It didn't take much exposure to the truth to get them to turn on one another though. He could see their true thoughts and fears, but Sienna's illusions only added credibility to his words. This small town was boring, but they were able to have some fun with these locals.

"Er-hem," a voice said from behind Cal, startling him.

He turned to find the young sheriff staring curiously at him. He didn't hear any footsteps. The sheriff's hands were hidden behind his back.

"Mind if we have a quick talk, man to man?" the sheriff said.

Cal's eyes darted around. Sienna was nowhere nearby and he hadn't seen Deacon for a few hours now. There were only a few townsfolk passing by. He couldn't escape.

He clenched his jaw and shook his head vigorously. "I've got nothing to say to you, sir."

He turned on his heel and started to make his way toward the inn, but suddenly felt something hard strike his head. He stumbled forward, using one hand to steady himself and touching the back of his head with the other hand. He could feel something warm and wet on the back of his skull.

As Cal fell, he managed to turn to one side, keeping one hand on his head and breaking his fall with his free hand. He looked back to see the young sheriff standing in the same place, with a fist-sized rock hovering next to him, flecked with blood.

"You may not have anything to say to me directly, but you and your gang have a lot to answer for," Wiz said before allowing the projectile to sail toward the pale man.

Cal attempted to shield his face, only for the telekinetically-propelled missile to dart to one side and smash into his temple with a sickening *crunch*.

Wiz scanned the area. He'd instructed the Winchester women to lead the other members of the Four Revenants down a longer route to the saloon. He knew they must have succeeded.

The people in the street nearby watched, horrified by what they had just witnessed, unsure of what to do. Wiz nodded to them, "It's alright, folks. I'm just catching another outlaw. Please go on about your day, head on home and do not speak of this for your own safety. The Winchesters will provide further instructions."

Once the small group of onlookers dispersed, Wiz levitated himself slightly from the ground while holding the unconscious man by the ankles. He floated backwards toward the alley, dragging the deadweight with him. He wished he could just move the lump of a man with a thought, but his power had no effect. Deacon told the truth about their abilities being useless against others with gifts.

Being able to levitate did give Wiz the benefit of not straining his legs to move the body through town, but his arms would not be so lucky. An old tarp hanging nearby would suffice to wrap Cal up and move him to the backdoor of Wesley's drinkery. He arrived at the old building and knocked on the door. Wesley opened the door slowly. The pistol once carried by Sienna was in one of his hands. The acrid odor of gunpowder from inside the storage room greeted Wiz's nose before he stepped inside.

"They're both here," Wesley said. "And they don't seem to be onto us yet."

"Good," Wiz said, pulling Cal's body over to a scorched open crate full of melted guns. It was his first time seeing the weapons, but he did not bother giving them a second thought. He had what was necessary now and he needed to focus on the task to come.

Deacon noticed the odor of gunpowder once he entered the front door to the saloon.

"Smells like the sheriff must've had some fun playing in your daddy's secret room," Deacon said to Whitney.

She glanced at him, her face expressionless now. "Excuse me. I have to return home to tend to my father now," she said making her way back out the door.

Deacon chuckled as he watched her leave and called after her as he took a seat at one of the tables, "Give him my regards and you feel free to stop by that inn any time. Or perhaps I may visit you!"

Upon his last word, Sienna burst through the door. Deacon could see the medicine woman behind her, stopping outside of the entrance and following her daughter away from the place.

"Oh... Deacon," Sienna said. "Surprise seeing you and only you here. I thought I was meeting the little lawman, but didn't expect to see the whole place cleared out like this."

Deacon smirked and waved her forward. "I guess this is meant to be a private gathering to celebrate him as a new addition to our family."

"I'm guessing you didn't give him much of a choice in the matter," Sienna said with a giggle, taking a seat next to him.

 "I did give him two choices though," Deacon said. "I guess someone will be bringing Cal here, too."

"Sure smells funny in here," Sienna said sniffing the air.

"Yeah," Deacon said, standing and making his way behind the bar to grab two bottles of moonshine from a shelf. "The sheriff must've destroyed the barkeep's stash of weapons and gunpowder once I informed him of our little discovery. We're probably just smelling the bits of whatever's left here. I wouldn't worry. Let's get the fun started while we wait for the sheriff and Cal."

Wiz covered the pistol confiscated from one of Revenants with his shirt and readjusted his clothes to better conceal it before making his way into the barroom. He hated the feel of the cold metal resting against his skin, but he knew having the weapon tucked in his waistband was a necessary precaution in case things didn't go as planned.

Deacon and Sienna were already laughing and talking loudly, slightly slurring their words. Two empty bottles sat on the table in front of them. They both waved when they spotted him.

Wiz strode over to the pair, using his abilities to lift multiple bottles from the shelves to make them drift to the table before he took his seat.

"Why, hello again, little lawman," Sienna said, playfully fluttering her eyelids.

"I take it you've considered my offer, brother?" Deacon said.

"Very straightforward," Wiz said, smirking and uncapping a bottle of whiskey. "Yes, I did consider it and we have much to discuss and celebrate."

Wiz passed the open bottle to Deacon, who immediately set the bottle down on the table.

"So... what say you, brother?" Deacon asked, looking Wiz over suspiciously. "I can wait for Cal to arrive before we drink any more, but I can't wait to hear your answer."

"Cal, wasn't invited to this shindig, so no need to wait," Wiz replied. "Feel free to drink up. We have plenty of time to talk."

"Well, if I can't get an answer from you now, maybe I should make a visit to the barkeep, the barmaid and the medicine woman in the meantime," Deacon said, rising from his seat with a wicked grin spreading on his wide face. "The little lady was making eyes at me on the way here. I think we could get closer if

I'm staying in town longer. I can also punish that barkeeper some more if you'd like."

Wiz stood to his feet reaching out to put a hand on Deacon's left shoulder to urge him to sit, but then…

BANG!

The single shot rang out and Deacon spun to one side, falling back into his chair. His right shoulder was bleeding.

Wesley stepped out from the backroom, smoking pistol in hand and still raised to fire another shot at Deacon.

"You spineless little bar snake!" Sienna said, trembling with anger but remaining in her own seat.

"Wesley, what are you doing?" Wiz demanded. "This is not how this should go!"

"This was always how it was going to go after he burned me and threatened my family!" Wesley shouted.

Deacon snapped his fingers, lighting his fingertips.

Wesley laughed. "Go ahead and blow us all up. Almost every foot of this place is covered in gunpowder. By the time you throw a ball of flame at me, the whole place will be lit up like kindling for a campfire. You'd just be saving me the bullets."

Deacon waved his hand and the flames disappeared. "I guess you think you've got me cornered, huh?" He smirked and glanced over at Wiz. "You were the one who concocted this plan, ay, sheriff?"

"As a matter of fact, I came up with the plan to get you here, but this wasn't exactly it," Wiz said.

Deacon laughed. "You keep putting your trust in the wrong man, brother. One more reason you should have chosen to rule with us on your side... but now you just get to die with him!"

"No one is dying, not if you want to leave here with Cal," Wiz said.

Deacon and Sienna both straightened up, both of their eyes fixed on Wiz. Wesley walked a little closer to the table where the group was seated but maintained a safe distance with his gun still trained on Deacon.

"Where is he?" Deacon demanded

"He's in the back with a nasty concussion," Wesley said. "If you try to blow us apart you take him with us. Not that you'll get the chance."

"No, Wesley, they do get a chance," Wiz said, keeping his eyes on the pair seated next to him. "Having power or a weapon to put someone at your mercy does not make you a judge. And even if they wrong you, you aren't administering justice. You're just vengeful."

"So, what if I am?" Wesley shrugged.

"You're a better man than that, Wesley," Wiz said. "They've all had great harm done to them and witnessed losses. Hurt people hurt other people. I understand that." Turning back to Deacon and Sienna, he said, "I took away guns from the townsfolk. I can't take away your powers. But I can give y'all a chance to leave here peacefully. Deacon, you can still choose to use your power for a greater purpose."

Deacon narrowed his eyes, silent for a moment, but finally saying, "I've made peace with who and what I am. I'm perfectly satisfied with my choice."

In that moment, the door to the storage room flung open and a disoriented Cal stumbled through, groaning.

Wesley turned, immediately startled at the sight of the now paler man. Unfortunately, he forgot the gun was still in his hand as he turned and the surprise of Cal's appearance was all it took for him to tense up, gripping the trigger. The gunshot went straight through Cal's temple, opposite of where Wiz bludgeoned him with the rock.

"NO!" Sienna shrieked as Cal's now lifeless body slumped to the ground.

Before Wiz could react, Deacon launched himself from his chair tackling him to the ground and pinning him. "You can't move me with your mind, little sheriff, and you're not quite big enough to muscle your way out either."

Wiz raised one hand to attempt to push the larger man off, but Deacon proceeded to pound his face and chest with quick punches, forcing Wiz to recoil and hold his arms close to his body to defend himself.

Sienna charged at Wesley, who was still in shock at what he'd done, but managed to turn in time to raise his gun at her. She stopped in her tracks, raising her hands in surrender, but smirking. "It's unchivalrous to raise a weapon at an unarmed lady, sir. I may have had a drink, but are you sure you aren't the one who is drunk?"

The room suddenly felt like it was spinning for Wesley. His senses were distorted, his vision blurring and ears now ringing. The gun felt heavy in his hand and his legs felt like they were buckling beneath his own weight. He felt his arm drop to his side and thought he heard the pistol clatter on the floor, but he could not pinpoint where the noise came from or see clearly where it had fallen. He stumbled, catching his elbow on a nearby table to steady himself.

Sienna laughed as she picked up the dropped gun. She raised it toward Wesley's head. "A head for a head is always my motto."

Wiz spotted Sienna and the discombobulated Wesley. Despite the beating Deacon was giving him, he was able to concentrate just enough to will the gun to jerk to the side, flying from Sienna's hands and behind the bar. Sienna was temporarily startled and turned to give Wiz a nasty look before kicking Wesley in the side, knocking him to the ground.

"You're resilient, sheriff," Deacon said, continuing to swing down at Wiz, "but maybe you missed your calling by turning down the offer to join us."

"Doubtful," Wiz said, wriggling a bit to get his hips free and reaching down toward his waistband. "I believe everything happens for a reason, and I'm the type to plan for just about everything."

Wiz pulled the pistol free, tilting it just enough and firing a shot into Deacon's left knee.

Deacon cried in pain, rolling to one side and cradling his wounded leg.

Sienna was still viciously kicking Wesley who was rolling on the floor, still under the influence of her illusion. Wiz stood to his feet and fired a shot, grazing her shoulder. It was not enough to wound her as badly as Deacon, but apparently it distracted her and the pain broke her concentration enough to allow Wesley to regain his bearings.

Wesley shook his head and rubbed his eyes. He coughed a bit, winded from the relentless barrage of kicks to his abdomen. He pushed himself back to his feet.

Sienna began to say something, but Wesley immediately hit her with a haymaker that knocked out one of her teeth and sent her reeling back and falling to the floor, unconscious.

"Demons like you don't deserve chivalry," Wesley said, still huffing.

Deacon roared. Seeming to forget himself, his eyes appeared to suddenly light up. No flames erupted from his body, but instead Wesley's clothes instantly ignited!

"I forgot to mention, sheriff, I don't need to just throw flames. I can burn up anything I concentrate on from a distance!"

Wesley started flailing, doing his best to pat out the flames, but cautious to keep himself from falling to the gunpowder-covered floor.

Wiz used his power to fling the top off of a barrel Wesley kept in the corner of the bar, then lifting it and flipping it over at the center of the room. He knew it was filled with dirtied water, often used to clean up the vomit and other messes made by the frequent drunks, but it was his best option to douse the floor. He also made sure to spill some of the liquid on Wesley to put out flames on his clothes.

Wesley slumped against a table, unharmed for the most part and gasping from shock, but still gripping his gun.

"I doubt you have enough water to keep up with me, sheriff!" Deacon said, as a beam above Wiz burst into flame.

The beam cracked and collapsed. Wiz repelled it just moments before it could hit him, flinging it toward Deacon, who ducked as the burning wood crashed through the window behind him.

"Deacon, stop!" Wiz commanded. "The gunpowder is still scattered! You'll kill Sienna, too!"

Deacon simply laughed maniacally. His visage contorted into something Wiz could only imagine the biblical demons would look like. "In the story of Samson, he killed more of his enemies in death than he did when he lived. If you chose to leave with us, I would have burned this town to the ground anyway. Now, I just get to burn the place down around you!"

Sienna finally got back to her feet. Her fiery red hair soaked and something sticking to the side of her face. She brushed off the filth, disgusted. She still trembled with rage, her eyes wide and darting around the room between Deacon, Wiz, Wesley and the burning ceiling. She began to back away toward one of the walls, shaking her head and muttering something under her breath.

"Sienna, let's go!" Deacon said, limping toward the door.

"No!" Sienna shrieked. "You were about to kill me, too! *All of you!* All defilers! All destroyers!"

"Suit yourself, then!" Deacon yelled, snapping his fingers and throwing a stream of fire toward the ceiling and down the far wall near Wesley and Sienna.

Deacon then hobbled through the door as fast as he could, igniting the doorframe on his way out.

Sienna ran toward the door after him, with Wesley close on her heels. Another piece of burning debris fell toward the pair, but Wiz's power hurled it from them both. Wiz himself dodged a burning beam as he slid toward the table nearest the door, his pistol still tight in his grip. The flames on the walls were spreading quickly from floor to ceiling and making their way toward the storage room where the remaining gunpowder was set.

Wiz used his abilities to push a portion of the front wall out to clear a path near the main entrance. Once Sienna and Wesley were outside, he launched all of the tables in the bar toward the back of the barroom, flipping them on their side to form a barricade before backpedaling out as the building exploded. The barrier withheld some of the blast, but several pieces of splintered wood and glass bottles were propelled by the explosion. Wiz shielded himself with his powers from the projectiles that sped past him. A second smaller explosion blew out more burning debris.

Wiz barely heard the gasp from behind him. He turned to find Sienna gripping her side and throat, something jagged protruding from her abdomen and a piece of glass sticking from the side of her neck. Both of her pale hands were quickly stained red as the blood flowed between her fingers.

Chapter 9: Burnout

The sun was setting on the horizon, the last lights of the day fading, like the light in Sienna's eyes.

Wesley unconsciously reached out to catch the woman as she fell back. He looked down pityingly at her, mentally acknowledging her beauty despite her wicked actions, scarred face, and the repulsive smell of the water matting her hair. However, the stench was on him, too. They were no different in that regard. Then again, he could very well be scarred by the burns he suffered and he had been pushed to commit terrible acts himself today.

"You've done monstrous things..." Wesley said to the woman, but also speaking out loud to himself, with a hint of regret in his voice. "But I see a bit of my own daughter and my wife in you. I'm truly sorry for whatever made you follow that man. Maybe if you could've grown up here, things would've been different..."

Sienna mouthed something, but only managed to make a gurgling noise in her throat with the blood pooling and spilling from her mouth. Her eyes suddenly rolled up, her head fell to one side, and her hands dropped lifelessly to her sides.

Wesley looked up to Wiz and asked, "You're seeing this too, right?"

Wiz nodded. "Yeah. There's no illusion this time. I'm sorry about your saloon, by the way. We sacrificed the place for nothing it seems."

Wesley shook his head. "Not for nothing. We can still return one last devil back to hell."

Wiz looked down the street, suddenly horrified by the sights and sounds he now witnessed. He was previously distracted by the explosion of the saloon, but taking in the conflagration set on the whole town was disturbing. Several men and women with their own bodies ablaze screamed and rolled in the dust of the street. The porches, walls and roofs of multiple buildings burned, brightening the town against the dimming daylight. A stray horse with its tail ablaze ran past Wiz and Wesley, followed closely by another whose entire back was covered in flames, resembling a vehicle of the agents of the apocalypse.

"He's gone completely mad," Wesley muttered.

"This is just like the day my aunt and uncle died..." Wiz said, slowly walking down the path. His heart sank and his mind began to drift to that day, but he was brought back to the present by Wesley's voice.

"He's lighting the path toward where he's going... NO!" Wesley screamed running ahead and snatching the weapon from Wiz as he passed by. "I know where he's headed! We have to catch that demon now!"

Whitney and Esther huddled together on the living room couch.

"Mama, do you think Daddy is okay?" Whitney asked, barely able to contain the tremble in her voice.

"I pray so, but—" Esther began, but she was suddenly interrupted by three loud pounds on the front door of the home.

Esther rose and proceeded to cautiously approach the portal only for the door to suddenly explode inward. She was knocked off of her feet by the blast of fire and splintering wood. She fell to her back, shielding her face with her arms.

Once she was able to push herself up on one elbow, she felt a sudden chill run down her spine when she saw the tall, dark figure in the doorway. One piece of his left pants leg was torn away, revealing a cauterized wound over the kneecap. He limped slightly and there was fresh blood on one of his shoulders as well, but there was no lacking in his menacing presence.

"Hey!" Deacon yelled, cackling as he stalked toward the two women, tapping the holstered gun on his hip. "Your new daddy's home!"

Whitney ran forward to pull her mother back up to her feet. The two of them rushed to the door for the master bedroom, only for a wall of flame to suddenly rise to block their escape.

"Don't make me turn you into ash too soon," Deacon growled. "I had to stop by the sheriff's place to pick up my weapon, so that already cost me a few minutes, but we deserve some quality time now, don't you think? I mean, especially after your whole family cost me the entirety of my chosen family!"

Whitney stepped in front of her mother, eyeing Deacon defiantly. Esther tugged on her daughter's arm, trying to restrain her, but Whitney resisted, leaning closer toward Deacon.

"You deserve worse for what you did to my daddy!" Whitney shrieked.

"I deserve more than what this pathetic place could offer me!" Deacon yelled back, his eyes flashing as the ends of Whitney's hair suddenly ignited.

Whitney screamed patting the embers with her palms and stumbling back. Esther caught her daughter before she tripped and fell into the growing fire waiting by the bedroom. The older woman swiftly grabbed a cup of water from a table nearby and doused the teenager with the cup's contents. Esther quickly inspected the mildly singed hairs and light burns on Whitney's hands and clothes, but noting she was otherwise unharmed.

"I deserve more than this diseased, corrupt world can offer!" Deacon continued, stalking slowly toward the two women. "I don't know if the fire I summon is hellfire or heaven's flame, but whichever it is, it's enough to cleanse some of the world. This is my choice. This town isn't the first or the last, but it's enough for kindling the fire of—"

BANG!

Deacon twisted, arching backward, stumbling and groaning.

BANG!

Deacon fell to his knees.

Wesley stepped toward the wounded man who writhed on the floor clutching at the new wounds in his right shoulder and lower back.

"You should've never come to this home or this town, for that matter," Wesley said aiming his gun at Deacon's head.

BANG!

"Men with power go where they please, barkeep," Deacon said, gritting his teeth in a twisted grin and holding up his own smoking pistol.

"Daddy!" Whitney cried out.

"No..." Esther said quietly, her voice shaking.

Wesley doubled over, gripping the hole in his gut. Two more gunshots rang in the air and two more sharp pains ripped through Wesley's chest and abdomen. Whitney and Esther's cries could be heard, but they seemed to grow further away. He coughed and felt something warm and wet dribble down his chin and tasted copper in his mouth. The heat from the growing fire nearby began to peel away from his skin, replaced by a sudden coldness that seemed to creep from the inside out. His vision began to fade and his legs felt heavier than they had when he was under the witch Sienna's glamor. He closed his eyes and fell forward only seeing a white light behind his eyelids and hearing Wiz's voice calling to him from somewhere nearby, joining with the voices of his other loved ones.

"Wesley!" Wiz shouted, pushing the remains of the burning door to one side.

Deacon managed to get back to his feet, pointing his gun toward Esther and Whitney with one trembling hand and gripping his side with the other. "Sheriff... Welcome to the grand finale. Your barkeep tried to serve me his own brand of justice twice now. I'm only returning the favor!"

Wiz could see he was bleeding from fresh wounds and his breathing was labored. He could also see the wild look in Deacon's eyes, one like a wounded beast ready to chew off its own leg or throw itself off a cliff to escape hunters.

"I managed to stop the fires to most of the buildings, but you killed plenty of people in this town who had nothing to do with this."

Deacon shrugged, which looked odd with one chunk of his right shoulder now missing. "As their protector, every person in this town was *your responsibility*, sheriff. This whole ordeal was caused by the choices *you* made for this town. Therefore, everyone living here was already involved from the moment we met. I already told you that this town, and that included the people in it, could be ruled by us or burned to the ground. If you chose to leave to come with me and my group, then the people weren't worth keeping alive anyway. If you'd welcomed us as equals to stay, I would've gladly helped you protect the people if they followed our laws. But no... You chose to completely reject us. You treated us like we were beneath you, like the degenerative filth who made us what we are now. The same ones who treated us and our ancestors like we were less than human. "

As Deacon spoke, Wiz concentrated on the weapon in Deacon's grip and sent it flying across the room into the adjacent bedroom which was still blocked by the wall of flame.

"No," Wiz shouted. "You chose to abuse your gift and became worse than the people who wronged you."

Deacon roared and the surrounding fires leapt toward Wiz in response.

Wiz countered by using his power to rip up the floorboards, tearing down the roof, and pulling any nearby furniture to him, rapidly rotating the wood and upholstery around himself to create a spinning shield. The flames still licked at him but Wiz kept the burning debris at a safe distance to keep himself from suffering more severe burns.

"DUCK!" Wiz commanded.

Whitney and Esther immediately understood, diving to one side just as Wiz flung the mass of spinning materials toward Deacon. Deacon summoned a stream of fire from his hands, attempting to blast the telekinetically-propelled debris away and creating a massive explosion in front of him that blew away the remaining walls in front and to either side of him.

Deacon collapsed to his knees. His wounds and the strain of using his abilities finally taking their toll on his body. Smoke and dust swirled around him. He could not see the sheriff or the two women anywhere, but he could hear the women coughing nearby.

Even if I die here, I can burn this house to the ground with them inside or just incinerate their bodies, Deacon thought to himself. *The roof should be collapsing on all of us any moment now...*

"Hurry, run this way, you two!" the sheriff's voice called.

Deacon could see the silhouette of the young man through the smoke now. The sheriff had one empty hand raised over his head, apparently stabilizing the remains of the house with his gift. However, the other hand held the pistol he'd used in their earlier scuffle at the saloon, the same one the barkeep had just used to shoot him. The sheriff must have used the distraction of the spinning debris to also pull the weapon to himself.

Deacon smiled as the weapon flashed in the sheriff's hands. He gagged as the tremendous force of the small piece of lead pierced through the side of his neck.

Deacon's eyes tracked the figures of the two Winchester women running through the smoke. He could easily turn them both into kindling on two legs, and let the sheriff watch in dread as the last members of his own chosen family burned just out of his reach... However, the pain in his body was distracting, making it difficult to concentrate enough to summon the flames to them, but then Deacon had a better idea.

Wiz stepped closer toward Deacon, tears streaking his face now, cutting through the soot coating his cheeks as he clearly saw the charred remains of Wesley Winchester that were left in the explosion. Wiz's anger rose, but then he felt horrified once he saw Deacon, whose body glowed as white flames burst through his wounds and out of every orifice on his body. Deacon's eyes melted into his skull and his hair and clothing burned away, consumed by self-immolation. Even more eerily, he grinned the whole time as the fire from within ate away at him, until only the smoking bones were left behind.

Esther and Whitney slept in the sheriff's office overnight. After Wiz emerged from the burning home, they said nothing, but only held each other as the remaining walls collapsed.

There were several others whose homes were uninhabitable after the arsonist's rampage and at least ten dead. If Wiz had not stopped to help put out some of the fires, many more would have died, but if he'd confronted Deacon first, Wesley might have still been alive at least...

As the two women slept, Wiz gathered what food and supplies he could into a bag, including one of the pistols he'd confiscated from the Four Revenants. He hesitated before slipping the gun in with his other belongings, but considered the possibility of encountering others like Deacon once he set out. There were many unknowns on the path ahead.

He heard someone stirring behind him and turned to find Whitney sitting up in bed, watching him. Her mother remained asleep.

"Never thought I'd see you so comfortable with a gun," Whitney said quietly, smirking.

"Yeah... me either," Wiz said, trying to avoid her eyes in the low light of the room. The first beams of the rising sun were coming through the window, settling on the space between them. "I always hated these things. I still do. I've lost too many family members to people using them."

"But even you have use for them now that you know what else is out there, huh? Not as powerful as you thought you were?" Whitney said, standing now and stepping closer toward him, the light streaking her face.

Wiz looked at her closely. Her green eyes were brighter than he thought. She seemed much more mature now. He wondered if it was from the exhaustion, sadness and weariness weighing on her features that aged her so much. He was impressed anyone could sleep last night after all they'd been through. He could not.

"Are you able to read minds now, too?" Wiz asked, raising an eyebrow but barely able to crack a smile.

"No, but I'm able to read people from what I see with my own eyes," Whitney said. "I think it's a talent I picked up from my daddy."

Wiz looked away from her again, feeling a pang of sadness deepen at the mention of Wesley. "I'm sorry. I cared about everyone in this town, but I cherished you Winchesters most of all. You've lost your bar, your home and your father…"

"And now we're all losing our sheriff, too."

"Yes, but you don't need me. I don't need to be sheriff. Deacon and Wesley were both right to some degree. I did take away everyone's chance to protect themselves. I was foolish and arrogant. I had some part in the destruction of this place."

Whitney shrugged. "But you were right too. I've seen a lot of things growing up here, working at daddy's business. You also protected a lot of them from themselves…”

“Maybe so…”

“Just one question. Why didn’t you kill that man sooner? I understand your power couldn’t touch him like McGraw, but you could have done something to stop him before.”

Wiz’s eyes teared up as his gaze met hers. He could hear the hurt in her voice and the truth inside of him hurt him even more, but it had to be spoken. “I hesitated because I felt connected to Deacon. I kind of understood his pain and anger, because I’ve felt it every day I remember what happened to my aunt and uncle, and when I imagine what might have happened to my own ma. I disagreed with him, but I understood him. I thought I could get through to him, but he was worse than McGraw. Feeling powerful, with a gun or a gift from God, makes most men dangerous.”

“So you removed guns from this town first and now you’re removing yourself, our own guardian angel?”

"Wisdom Peak can have its guns back. The new sheriff can make that call. I think I need to find a purpose outside of this place, allow myself to grow and allow the town to grow without me. I'm no angel, any more than Deacon was a demon. God will still be here to protect the people I love, no matter where on earth or in the afterlife I go."

Whitney ran up and embraced Wiz tightly. He hugged her back, feeling a sudden weight lift from his conscience and body. Was this forgiveness? He let the tears fall down his cheek and could feel her trembling and his shirt getting wet as she buried her face into his chest. They stood there for what felt like an hour, continuing to hold each other.

The sun was getting higher. Wiz finally stepped away from Whitney and she let him go. He shouldered his bag and stepped quietly toward the door. He was anticipating Esther to wake up at any moment, but he wanted to get out of town before he had to endure anymore tearful goodbyes.

No one needed to know where Wiz would go next. He intended to let the small voice that moved his spirit to guide him to wherever he was needed. He had a purpose to fulfill, and though much was lost in the last twenty-four hours in Wisdom Peak, there was much to be discovered beyond it.

Once he set foot outside, Wiz looked to the skies and concentrated, allowing himself to be propelled upward. The dust from the streets of the town he had called home for so many years fell free from his boots as he ascended over it, but unlike the night he lost Jean and Laverne and revealed his true self, he refused to look down upon Wisdom Peak or look back as he flew away.